JANE YOLEN

How Do Dinosaurs

Stay Friends?

Illustrated by

MARK TEAGUE

SCHOLASTIC INC.

This book was originally published in hardcover
by The Blue Sky Press in 2016.

ISBN 978-1-338-11402-7

Text copyright © 2016 by Jane Yolen.
Illustrations copyright © 2016 by Mark Teague.
All rights reserved. Published by Scholastic Inc.,
Publishers since 1920. SCHOLASTIC and
associated logos are trademarks and/or
registered trademarks of Scholastic Inc.

12 11 10 9 8 7 6 5 4 3 2 1   16 17 18 19 20 21

Printed in the U.S.A.   40

First Scholastic paperback printing, September 2016

Book design by Kathleen Westray

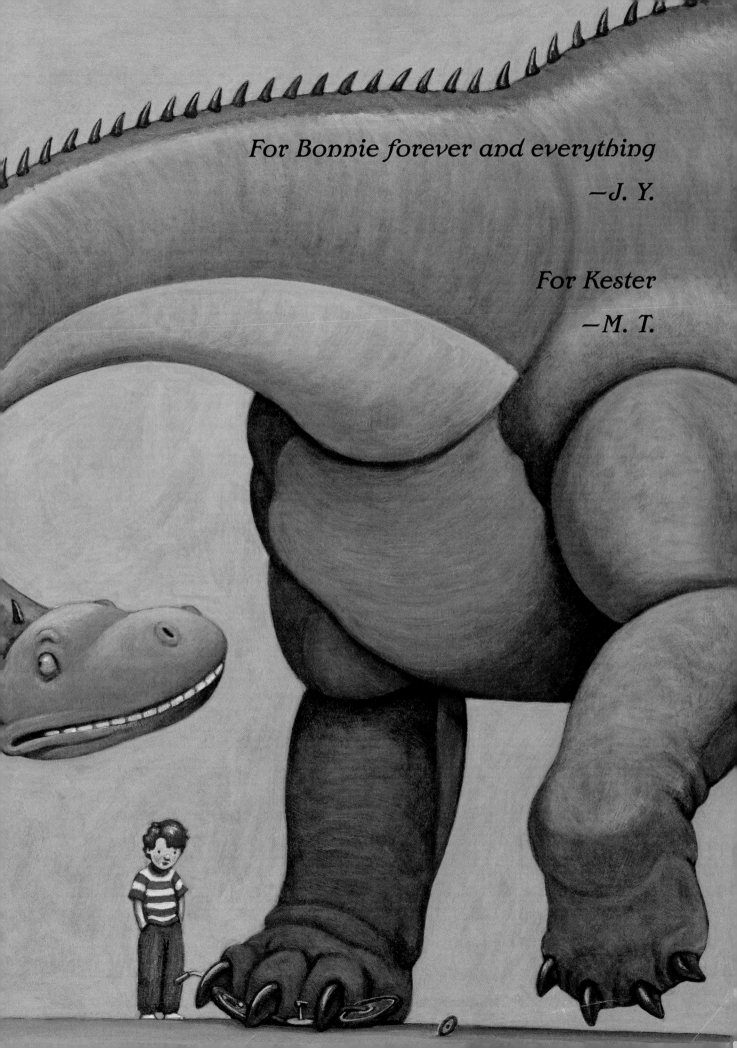

For Bonnie forever and everything
—J. Y.

For Kester
—M. T.

How does a dinosaur keep his best friend when a terrible fight just might signal the end?

ACROCANTHOSAURUS

Does he scribble
a note with a
horrible scowl?

Does he wipe
muddy feet on his
friend's favorite towel?

Does he tear up a book
that his friend
let him take?

Does he
throw his

friend's
lunch box
straight
into the
lake?

Does he write on the blackboard a very bad name?

Bb Cc Dd Ee Ff G

DILONG
IS
STUPID

DILONG

Does he tell all the kids
that his friend is to blame?

Does he kick
his friend's bike?

Does he egg
his friend's door?

Does he push his friend
hard so he lands
on the floor?

Does he tell the new teacher
a very big lie
about who did the pushing—
and why?

No . . . a dinosaur doesn't.
He won't even try.

He sends a nice note taking
most of the blame.
He's surprised when he finds
that his friend
did the same.

He has his friend over to share
and to play,

letting him choose

the first toys

of the day.

He brings to the school
a toy dragon
and knight,

with a card that says,
"Really, I don't
want to fight."

And then
when the class
is all given
a break,

he gives his friend
cookies
he helped his mom
make.

He wraps up a favorite bear
with a bow,
and he brings it along
as a gift,
just to show . . .

. . . that even though friends may occasionally fight,

there is always

a way to make

everything

right.

Good hugs and more

keep a friend, dinosaur.